4

5

6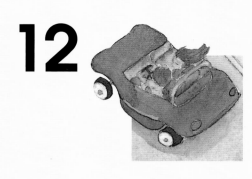

10

11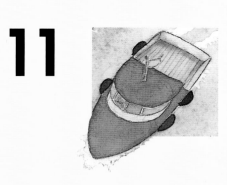

12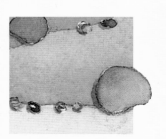

16

17

18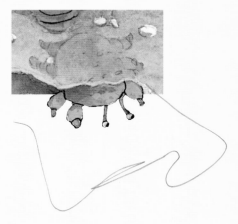

"Who can count every grain of sand on the beach
and all the stars in the sky?"

A Gull's Story
Part 2

Mayai Moare

For Jeffry and James

Counting at the Shore

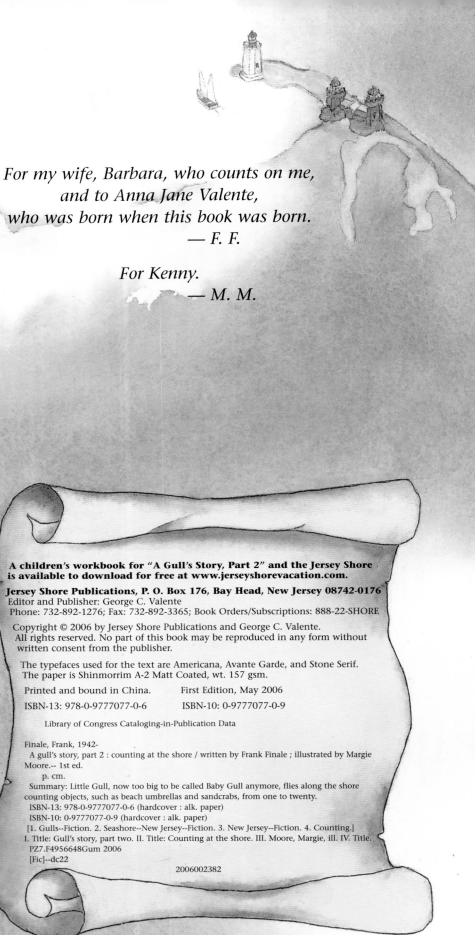

For my wife, Barbara, who counts on me,
and to Anna Jane Valente,
who was born when this book was born.
— F. F.

For Kenny.
— M. M.

A children's workbook for "A Gull's Story, Part 2" and the Jersey Shore
is available to download for free at www.jerseyshorevacation.com.

Jersey Shore Publications, P. O. Box 176, Bay Head, New Jersey 08742-0176
Editor and Publisher: George C. Valente
Phone: 732-892-1276; Fax: 732-892-3365; Book Orders/Subscriptions: 888-22-SHORE

The typefaces used for the text are Americana, Avante Garde, and Stone Serif.
The paper is Shinmorrim A-2 Matt Coated, wt. 157 gsm.

Printed and bound in China.   First Edition, May 2006

ISBN-13: 978-0-9777077-0-6   ISBN-10: 0-9777077-0-9

Library of Congress Cataloging-in-Publication Data

Finale, Frank, 1942-
  A gull's story, part 2 : counting at the shore / written by Frank Finale ; illustrated by Margie
Moore.-- 1st ed.
      p. cm.
  Summary: Little Gull, now too big to be called Baby Gull anymore, flies along the shore
counting objects, such as beach umbrellas and sandcrabs, from one to twenty.
  ISBN-13: 978-0-9777077-0-6 (hardcover : alk. paper)
  ISBN-10: 0-9777077-0-9 (hardcover : alk. paper)
  [1. Gulls--Fiction. 2. Seashore--New Jersey--Fiction. 3. New Jersey--Fiction. 4. Counting.]
  I. Title: Gull's story, part two. II. Title: Counting at the shore. III. Moore, Margie, ill. IV. Title.
  PZ7.F4956648Gum 2006
  [Fic]--dc22
                              2006002382

A Gull's Story
Part 2
Counting at the Shore

written by Frank Finale

illustrated by Margie Moore

Jersey Shore Publications • Bay Head, New Jersey

Once again, the Gull Family awoke on the beach. Mama Gull lovingly looked at Baby Gull and said to Papa Gull, "Our baby has grown and is no longer a baby. He is now our Little Gull."

Papa Gull smiled and agreed. "From now on, we'll call you Little Gull." Little Gull liked this, as he knew he was no longer a baby.

Papa Gull encouraged, "Now that you're a little older, go out on your own and explore more of the Shore and practice your counting. Use the numbers we taught you, but don't fly too far."

And Little Gull, as happy as a gull could be, did just that. He swooped up above the sea and then spotted a shadow in the water below. He dove down to take a look and began to count.

1 Peeking below a wave, Little Gull spots the shape of **one** dark shark swimming towards him. With a loud *"Squawk!"* he flies away.

2 On a high hill above the harbor, Little Gull sees **two** stone towers with lights that stare at the sea. These are the Twin Lights of Navesink.

3 Through the fog in the channel, he hears one, two, **three** buoys bonging and clanging on the waves.

4 Later, sun shines off the bay as Little Gull flies over **four** cormorants perched on pilings, each hanging its wings out to dry.

5 Little Gull lands on wet sand where he discovers **five** starfish, each with **five** pointed arms.

6 Little Gull is hungry. He flies over the crowded boardwalk and sees **six** people standing near a hot dog stand. He snatches a piece of hot dog roll from a girl's paper plate and flies off. *"Thank you,"* he squawks.

7 Floating in the wind over the ocean, he notices **seven** seahorses bobbing under the waves.

8 On the beach, he counts **eight** surf fishermen standing with their poles and pails.

9 On his way back to the bay, he comes upon five marsh snails and four more close by, **nine** in all.

10 Flying over Barnegat Bay, he counts **ten** sailboats racing with the wind.

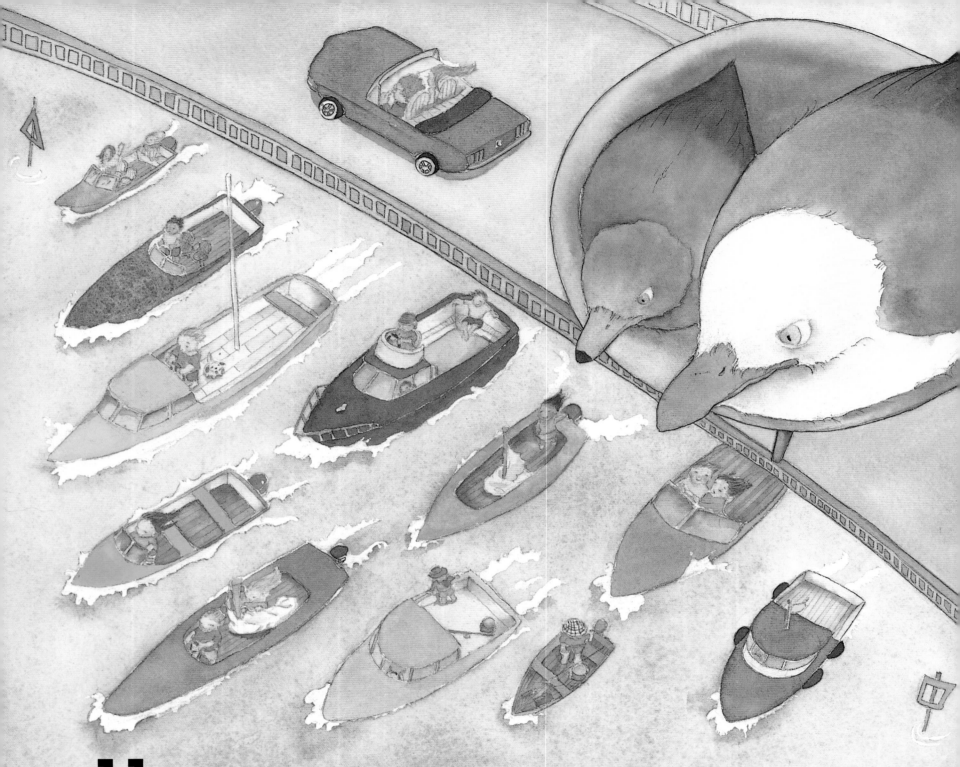

11 Resting atop a lamppost over a bridge, Little Gull meets Tuck, a craggy old gull, who is happy to see him. Together they count **eleven** boats that glide under the bridge...

12 …and **twelve** cars that zoom over the bridge to the seashore.

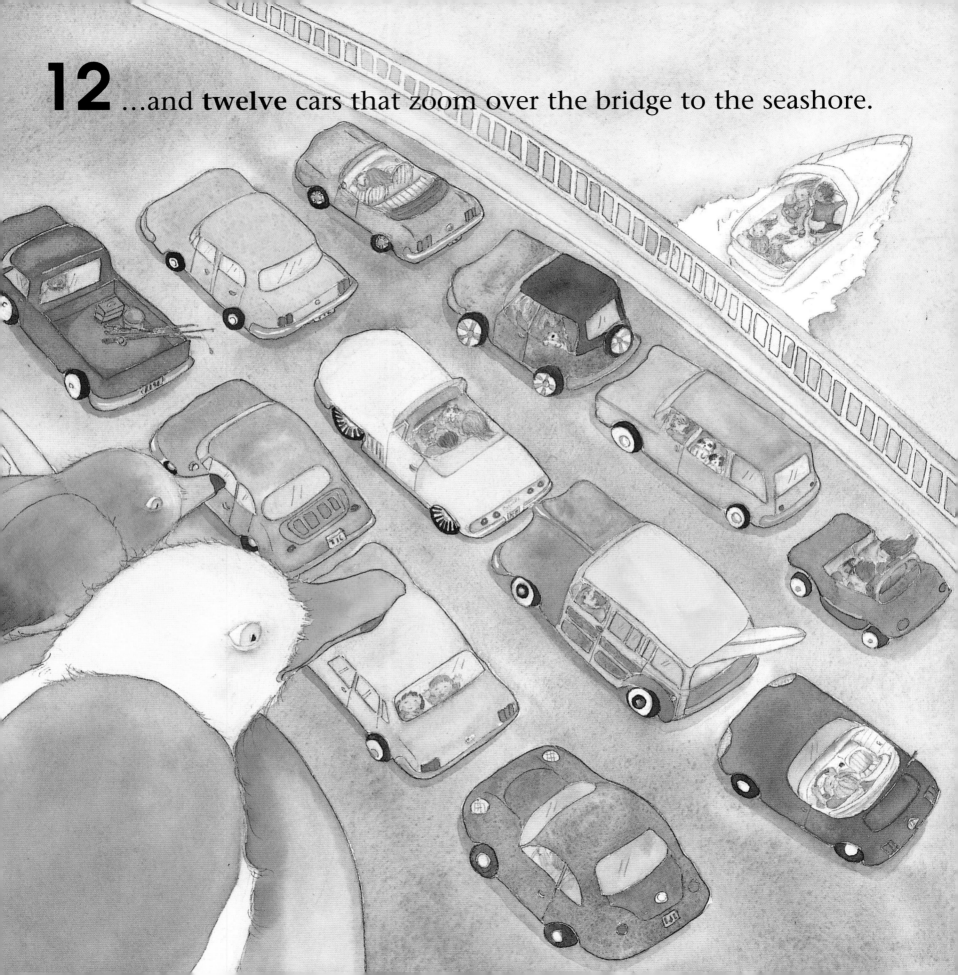

13 As they fly together, Tuck introduces Little Gull to a large sunfish lolling in the waves. Little Gull counts **thirteen** squid swimming nearby. It's getting late, so Little Gull says *"Goodbye"* to his new friend and continues his number journey home.

14 Back over the beach, he flies over **fourteen** bright beach umbrellas.

15 On seaside goldenrod, Little Gull counts **fifteen** monarch butterflies.

16 Little Gull hops down to the shore and sees **sixteen** surfers riding the waves. One of the surfers yells, *"Cowabunga!"* Little Gull squeaks back.

17 Walking along the shoreline, the glitter of sea-glass catches his eye. He counts **seventeen** smooth pieces.

18 Then Little Gull sees **eighteen** sandcrabs scuttling in the wash. This makes him hungry. Not too many to gobble, he thinks.

19 Little Gull hears sandpipers. He sees **nineteen** flitting in and out of the surf.

20 Hopping through flotsam and jetsam washed up along the beach, Little Gull comes upon **twenty** ladybugs snuggling on a tangle of sea grasses.

They must be tired, he thought. After a day of counting, Little Gull was feeling tired too.

Back home that night, as he was falling asleep, Little Gull thought
about his day and of the sea and sand and sky surrounding him.

As he began to dream, he longed to know, "Who can count every grain of sand on the beach and all the stars in the sky?"

Other titles from Jersey Shore Publications

Books
To The Shore Once More
To The Shore Once More, Volume II
A Gull's Story
Dick LaBonté, Paintings of the Jersey Shore and More
Ceramic Tile In 20th Century America
Spring Lake, Revisited
All Summer Long
The Poets of New Jersey
Long Beach Island Rhapsody

Magazines and Guidebooks
Jersey Shore Home & Garden
Jersey Shore Vacation Magazine
Jersey Shore Vacation Map
Long Beach Island Vacation Guidebook & Map
Jersey Shore Magazine & Guide

To order a book or subscription, please call (888) 22-SHORE
or visit www.jerseyshorevacation.com.

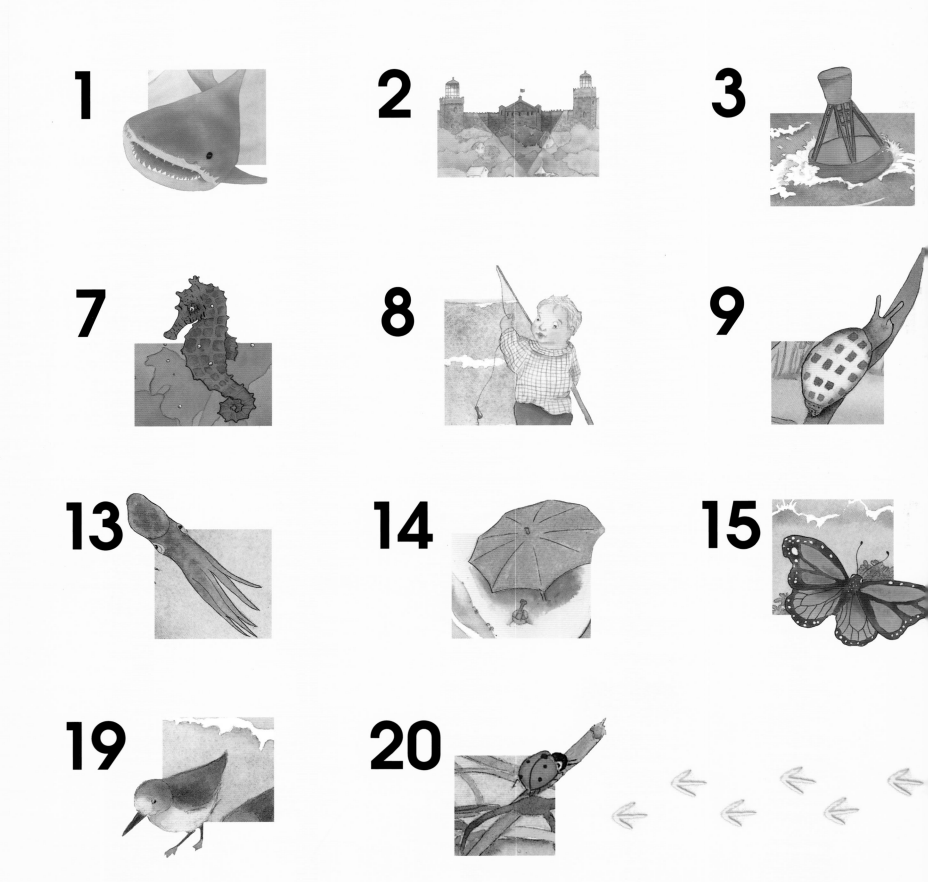